In My Backyard

In My Backyard

John DeVries

Werner Zimmermann

Scholastic Canada Ltd.

Scholastic Canada Ltd.
123 Newkirk Road, Richmond Hill, Ontario, Canada L4C 3G5

Scholastic Inc.
730 Broadway, New York, NY 10003, USA

Ashton Scholastic Pty Limited
PO Box 579, Gosford, NSW 2250, Australia

Ashton Scholastic Limited
Private Bag 1, Penrose, Auckland, New Zealand

Scholastic Publications Ltd.
Villiers House, Clarendon Avenue, Leamington Spa,
Warwickshire CV32 5PR, UK

6 5 4 3 2 1   Printed in Hong Kong   2 3 4 5 6/9

Canadian Cataloguing in Publication Data

De Vries, John
 In my backyard

ISBN 0-590-73681-7 (little bk.)

I. Zimmermann, Werner. II. Title

PS8557.E87I5   1992a   jC813'.54   C91-094326-5
PZ7.D48In 1992a

To Wanita
John

To Mupps, all heart and understanding.
And to Klaus, without whose frog this book
could not have been.
Werner

In my backyard I have a frog.

2

My mother found him on a log.

I called my frog my good friend Jim.

My mummy yelled, "Get rid of him!"

I asked my dad if Jim could stay.

6

My daddy said, "Take him away!"

I asked my grandpa if I could keep . . .

9

Oh, he's asleep.

I showed my sister my good friend Jim.
She nearly ran right over him!

So!

I told my dog (his name is Rover)

14

that he would soon be moving over.

And now Jim lives
with my dog in his house

16

with his cat and my mouse

with his bowl and my pail

with his box and my nail

with his rope and my ring

with his ball and my string

with his rug and my coat

with his tub and my boat

23

with his rod and my reel

with his rake and my wheel

with his pole and my flag

with his hole in my bag.

Rover, you're a pal!